Small Nose

Written by
Sarah Jane Lewis-Mantzaris
Illustrated by Stu McLellan

Collins

Who and what is in this story?

Listen and say

Ziggy the dog

Download the audio at www.collins.co.uk/839688

Jad

bush

hedgehog

Jad is playing with Ziggy the dog.

Catch, Ziggy!

The ball goes under the bush!

Ziggy finds two balls!

One ball is not a ball!
What is it, Ziggy?

Jad says, "Look, Mum! What is it?"
Mum says, "It's a hedgehog!"

Jad says, "Is it sleeping?"
Mum says, "No, it isn't."

Mum says, "Look at its small nose."
Jad can't see the hedgehog's eyes or ears.

Where is the hedgehog's face?

Jad says, "Let's give it some food."
Mum says, "OK, but it doesn't eat our food."

Jad wants to give the hedgehog some milk.

Mum says, "Hedgehogs don't drink milk."

Mum says, "Let's give it water and dog food."

Jad says, "You can have some too, Ziggy!"

Mum and Jad make a small house.
Mum says, "This is good."

Mum says, "Let's come back at night."

It's night. Jad and Mum are in the garden.

Mum says, "Look! I can see its face."

Jad says, "It's eating. It's got a small nose *and* a small mouth."

Jad is happy. He says to the hedgehog, "Your name is Small Nose."

Jad says, "I like having animals in our garden."

Picture dictionary

Listen and repeat

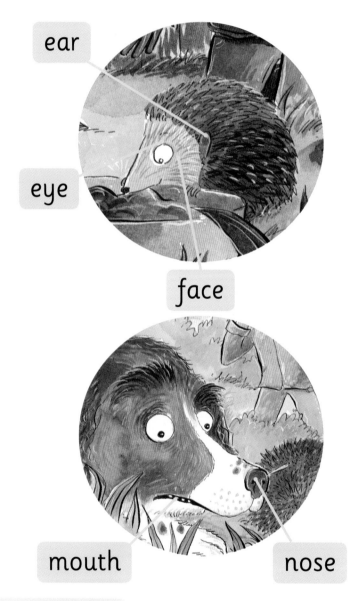

ear

eye

face

mouth

nose

1 Look and order the story

2 Listen and say

Collins

Published by Collins
An imprint of HarperCollins*Publishers*
Westerhill Road
Bishopbriggs
Glasgow
G64 2QT

HarperCollins*Publishers*
1st Floor, Watermarque Building
Ringsend Road
Dublin 4
Ireland

William Collins' dream of knowledge for all began with the publication of his first book in 1819.

A self-educated mill worker, he not only enriched millions of lives, but also founded a flourishing publishing house. Today, staying true to this spirit, Collins books are packed with inspiration, innovation and practical expertise. They place you at the centre of a world of possibility and give you exactly what you need to explore it.

© HarperCollins*Publishers* Limited 2020

10 9 8 7 6 5 4 3 2

ISBN 978-0-00-839688-6

Collins® and COBUILD® are registered trademarks of HarperCollins*Publishers* Limited

www.collins.co.uk/elt

British Library Cataloguing in Publication Data

A catalogue record for this publication is available from the British Library.

Author: Sarah Jane Lewis-Mantzaris
Illustrator: Stu McLellan (Beehive)
Series editor: Rebecca Adlard
Commissioning editor: Zoë Clarke
Publishing manager: Lisa Todd
Product managers: Jennifer Hall and Caroline Green
In-house editor: Alma Puts Keren
Project manager: Emily Hooton
Editor: Emma Wilkinson
Proofreaders: Natalie Murray and Michael Lamb
Cover designer: Kevin Robbins
Typesetter: 2Hoots Publishing Services Ltd
Audio produced by id audio, London
Reading guide author: Emma Wilkinson
Production controller: Rachel Weaver
Printed and bound by: GPS Group, Slovenia

MIX
Paper from
responsible sources

FSC
www.fsc.org

FSC™ C007454

This book is produced from independently certified FSC™ paper to ensure responsible forest management.

For more information visit: **www.harpercollins.co.uk/green**

Download the audio for this book and a reading guide for parents and teachers at www.collins.co.uk/839688